An Angel N...

ISBN 9780692460603
Published by Dream Hawk Media. (www.dreamhawkmedia.net)
Book Designer, Illustration Graphics, Emily Zieroth, Clair Montano and Mary Monette.

To my Angels—my Loving Husband Carey, my Angelic Mom Luz, my Talented Father Jaime, my Incredible Sister Angela, my Adorable God Son Giovanni, my Inspirational Stepson Dillon and my Heartfelt Brother Mario. I give you thanks for inspiring me and shining your light so brightly on me.

Once upon a time, there was a little girl named Elsa.
She had so many gifts and talents that she
did not know what to do with them.
Her parents, Mom Luz and Dad Jaime,
loved her so much and knew she was very different.

One day they left her in the middle of the field to see
if anything special would happen.
Elsa was all alone in the big green field,
but she was not scared at all.

She started to whistle. All of the sudden butterflies surrounded her. There were also bunny rabbits, frogs, and birds.

She was so happy but she wanted more company.
She started to whistle stronger, louder, and longer.
Soon the entire field was full of animals.
Even dogs and cats came to her calling.

Elsa was amazed but she wanted to know
what that meant. How did she get this power?

When it began raining she did not want to get wet.
So she said, "Rain, go away now!"
And it stopped raining.

Right then and there she knew she could do anything she wanted.
She started singing and dancing, and all of her animal friends joined her.
Elsa loved to sing; it made her feel free like the animals.

As night time came around, she started to get cold.
The dogs looked at her and said, "I cannot help."
The cats looked at her and said, "Me neither."
The bunny rabbits and frogs looked down,
knowing they couldn't do anything.

But the birds said, "Let's fly around and see if some of our feathers will fall down to the ground."

The birds flew faster and faster all around
the field. They sang as if they were having a party.
They were so loud, more and more birds came,
even eagles and hawks, big birds with big feathers.

They flew all around her. Tons of feathers fell down.
Elsa could not believe her eyes.
She took all the feathers, big and small,
and made wings out of them.

She used the branches from the tree to tie them together. Before she knew it, she had made two big wings.
She covered the wings over her like a blanket.
She looked up to the stars and said,
"Thank you angels! Thank you birds!"
"Good night all and I will see you in the morning."
She fell asleep and morning came quickly.

Elsa opened her eyes and said,
"The feathers are gone, and so are the animals."
She was all alone.
She felt something heavy on her back.
"Oh, there you are feather wings.
To her amazement the wings where attached
to her back. She heard a loud voice in her ear.
"Go ahead and fly."

Wow, she thought. I can fly?

She started running and jumping and trying to fly, but nothing happened. Then she said," I can fly. I will fly." She flapped her wings. Her feet lifted from the ground and she was flying.

She flew all around the field and she was so happy.
She wanted to show her family,
so she flew to her house where her mom
and dad lived.

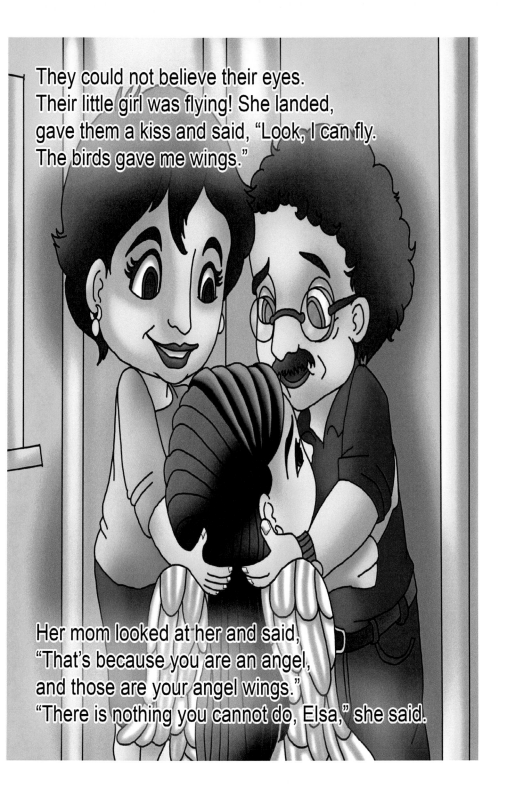

They could not believe their eyes.
Their little girl was flying! She landed,
gave them a kiss and said, "Look, I can fly.
The birds gave me wings."

Her mom looked at her and said,
"That's because you are an angel,
and those are your angel wings."
"There is nothing you cannot do, Elsa," she said.

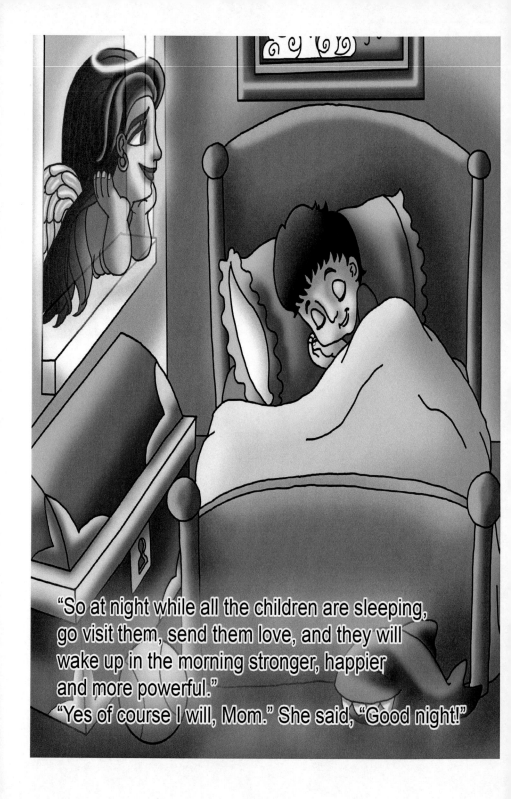

"So at night while all the children are sleeping, go visit them, send them love, and they will wake up in the morning stronger, happier and more powerful."

"Yes of course I will, Mom." She said, "Good night!"

Angela reading a book to Giovanni while
Elsa sends them love.
Angela tells him, "Angels are real and
are always with you!"

About the Author: Elsa J. Stokes is a best-selling author and motivational teacher. She has always been inspired to write since she was a little girl. You can find out more about her at www.AngelHealingWings.com..

This book was based on Elsa's amazing gifts and how she truly can make the rain go away. The characters in the page are also based on real people. Angela and Giovanni are Elsa's relatives. Angela is her sister, and Giovanni is her God Son. Her Mom Luz and Dad Jaime are also mentioned. See images below.

Angela & Giovanni

Luz & Jaime

The End!